TRICKY NELLY'S BIRTHDAY TREAT

It's Tricky Nelly Nickleby's birthday – and Billy the Bamboozler's got a special tricky treat in store for her!

Berlie Doherty is a highly regarded and prolific author for children. She has twice won the Carnegie Medal – for *Granny Was a Buffer Girl* and *Dear Nobody* – and was Highly Commended for *Willa and Old Miss Annie*. Her other Walker books are *Fairy Tales*, the picture book *The Midnight Man*, and the anthology *Tales of Wonder and Magic*. She has also written a volume of poetry, *Walking On Air*, as well as a number of plays, and adapted her own books for television, radio and theatre.

Books by the same author

The Magical Bicycle
Our Field
The Nutcracker
Old Father Christmas
Paddiwak and Cosy
The Midnight Man
Fairy Tales
Tales of Wonder and Magic
The Famous Adventures of Jack
Zzaap and the Word Master
Bella's Den
The Golden Bird
Willa and Old Miss Annie
Tilly Mint Tales
Coconut Comes to School
Blue John

Berlie has also written novels for older children. To
find out about all her books you can look up her
website: www.berliedoherty.com

Berlie Doherty

Tricky Nelly's Birthday Treat

Illustrations by Tony Ross

WALKER BOOKS
AND SUBSIDIARIES
LONDON · BOSTON · SYDNEY · AUCKLAND

For the Sumacs

First published 2003 by
Walker Books Ltd, 87 Vauxhall Walk
London SE11 5HJ

This edition published 2004

2 4 6 8 10 9 7 5 3 1

Text © 2003 Berlie Doherty
Illustrations © 2003 Tony Ross

The right of Berlie Doherty and Tony Ross to be identified
respectively as the author and illustrator of this work
has been asserted by them in accordance with the
Copyright, Designs and Patents Act 1988

This book has been typeset in Garamond

Printed in Great Britain by J.H. Haynes & Co. Ltd

British Library Cataloguing in Publication Data:
a catalogue record for this book
is available from the British Library

ISBN 1-84428-120-5

www.walkerbooks.co.uk

Contents

Chapter One

Some people said that it was the silliest thing in the world when Tricky Nelly Nickleby and Billy the Bamboozler ended up living in the same house together.

They couldn't help playing tricks on each other. It was in their bones, you see. Nelly loved to make a silly out of Billy and Billy loved to make a noodle out of Nelly.

But the silliest time of all was
when the Egg Man was brought
into it.

It happened because of Nelly's
birthday. She wanted a feather hat.
She'd seen one at the market and
she had to have it.

"Billy," Nelly said, "if you weren't so mean, I'd ask for the big black and red hat. But as you are, the little red one will have to do."

When she told him how much it was, he went sickly pale and gulped very hard. Although his pockets and socks were bulging with coins he couldn't bear to part with any of them.

So off Billy trudged, up the lane
in the rain with his collar turned up
and his hands saying goodbye to
the coins in his pockets. And what
should he see but two hens
walking towards him. One was
speckled and one was black.

Just the thing, he thought. I'll take the hens home and I'll pluck them. I'll stick the feathers on one of her old hats. She'll never know the difference. And we'll have chicken stew for her birthday tea, and I'll still have all my money. He couldn't have been more delighted.

He was walking back down the lane with a hen tucked under each arm, when who should he meet but the Egg Man, puffing like a fish.

"I see you've found my hens,"
the Egg Man panted. "I've been
looking for them all day."

"Oh, these aren't your hens," said Billy, quick as a rabbit. "They just look like them. I've just bought these at the market."

"Then you've come home the long way," said the Egg Man, "because the market was yesterday."

"Just bought them yesterday," agreed Billy, "and today I'm taking them round to show them the neighbourhood."

And back he went to his house,
leaving the Egg Man with his
mouth hung open and his hands
on his hips.

Nelly was upstairs, trying on her dowdy old hat for the very last time. "You'll be beautiful tomorrow, my girl," she crowed.

She heard Billy come in and ran downstairs. Quick as a flash he opened the door of the grandfather clock and shoved the hens inside.

"Where's my new hat?" she demanded.

"I've hidden it," he said. "It's not your birthday till tomorrow."

Silly Nelly Nickleby! She spied a little curled-up feather on the floor and her heart fluttered in her chest.

Chapter Two

cluck
cluck
cluck
cluck

But in the middle of dinner there came a muffled clucking and chuttering from inside the grandfather clock.

"Good gracious, what's that?" asked Nelly.

"Clock needs oiling," said Billy.

"Cluck," went the clock. "Churr-cluck."

When Billy
wasn't looking,
Nelly put two eggs
on the rug in front
of the grandfather
clock.

"Billy," she said,
"isn't it a wonderful
thing? We have a
grandfather clock
that lays eggs."

"Eggs?" he said.
"Well I never!"

Silly Billy!

And if he was
puzzled, he didn't
show it.

That night, as soon as Nelly had gone to sleep, Billy got the hens out of the clock and that was the end of them, poor things. Then he plucked them clean and glued the feathers all over Nelly's shabby old hat. They stuck up like fur on a frightened cat.

Nelly danced down the stairs next morning, eager for her present.

"Oh Billy!" she cooed. "The expensive one!"

And if she was puzzled, she didn't show it.

Billy's heart filled up with pride. He almost believed he had paid for the hat himself, until he remembered the hens.

"And there's a couple of chickens for us to cook," he told her, "for your birthday tea."

"Wait till I show the neighbours," said Nelly, and off she went with her new hat bold on her head and feathers floating round her like the falling leaves of autumn.

Chapter Three

The first person Nelly met was the
Egg Man. "Those are my hens
you've got on your head!" he
shouted.

"Indeed they aren't," she said.
"Billy bought this hat for me
yesterday morning."

"That's a pack of lies," said the Egg Man, "because I saw him yesterday morning as plain as you please and he had a hen tucked under each arm."

"Well!" Nelly said. "Why on earth would Billy want to go stealing hens when we have a grandfather clock that lays eggs?"

The Egg Man hung open his mouth and stood with his hands on his hips.

"Every day," said Nelly, "as it strikes two o'clock."

She went back home, took off the hat, and said to Billy, "About half the village will be coming round at two o'clock to see our grandfather clock laying eggs." And she went out to the garden to pick some flowers. That'll teach him to play tricks on me, she thought.

But Billy was not going to let
Nelly make a silly out of him. He
got out a drill and made a hole in
the bottom of the grandfather
clock. He covered up the sawdust
with his boot when Nelly came in.

"They'll be coming in ten
minutes," she told him.

"It's all the same to me," said
Billy.

As soon as her back was turned, Billy whipped open the door of the grandfather clock, put two eggs inside and tried to step in. But however hard he tried he just couldn't do it.

"Five to two," said Nelly, "and I think they're coming up the lane."

They were indeed. Billy could
hear the trudge of their boots and
the eager shout of their laughter.
He was about to be made a fool of.

"I was just looking inside the clock," he said. "It'll never lay eggs unless it's wound, and I've dropped my key inside it. Will you have a look for me, Nelly?"

Silly Nelly Nickleby!

And Billy the Bamboozler shut the door on her.

Chapter Four

At that very moment in walked the
Egg Man, two farmers and their
dogs, the lady from the post office,
the baker's boy and a grandfather.
The rest had to look through the
window.

Nelly started beating on the door of the grandfather clock.

"Just about time," said Billy. "It's working up to it."

As the clock struck one the pendulum hit Nelly on the ear. She stepped aside, kicked one of the eggs, and out through the hole it rolled.

The Egg Man opened his mouth and put his hands on his hips. The rest of the crowd all gasped.

The clock struck
again. The
pendulum bumped
against Nelly, who
stepped to one
side, a bit sharp
this time, and out
came the second egg,
gluey and gooey and clotted with
bits of shell, but an egg all the same.

"That's it," said Billy. "You're
upsetting it now. Off you go!"
And off they went, full of marvel.

"Let me out!" shouted Nelly.

Billy opened the door of the grandfather clock and Nelly tried to step out. But plump little Nelly was stuck fast, like a parsnip in a pea pod.

She wriggled and twisted and cursed, but there was no denying that she was stuck. "You can't leave me here!" wailed Nelly. "Run and get a hammer and break up the clock."

"I can't do that," said Billy, "it's two hundred years old. I tell you what. If you go for a week without eating, I'll soon get you out. You'd better tell me how to cook those birds for my tea."

Now, Nelly was steaming with rage. Not only was she having to do without her birthday tea, but she was having to tell that lazy, wily, mingy, grabby meany of a bamboozler how to cook a chicken!

43

"Just cook one!" she shouted. Perhaps by the time she was thin, the other would still be fresh enough to eat. "Put it in a pan and cover it with sour milk."

"Sour milk? Are you sure?"

"Quite sure. Makes it creamy." Nelly smiled.

"And shake in a couple of drums of pepper."

She could hear Billy sneezing like billy-oh.

"And a handful of thistles. Very tasty."

She could hear him yelling out in the yard.

"Then leave it to simmer till half
past six."

Billy's fingers were stinging.

His eyes were flooding.

His nose was gushing.

His tummy was thundering.

At last, dinner was cooked.

He poured the stew into a bowl
and sat right in front of Nelly to eat
it. He lifted it up to his lips,
opened his mouth and poured it
down his throat.

Silly Billy!

With a roar he clutched at his tongue, clutched at his throat, clutched at his stomach. With a bellow he charged three times round the house, drank dry the water tub, plunged into the stream, slammed the clock door on Nelly's laughing face, and then went to bed to be ill.

Chapter Five

Silence settled. Billy stopped
groaning and dropped off to sleep.
Nelly stopped knocking on the clock
door and dozed. The fire in the
grate hushed down into ashes.
Slowly, stealthily, the window
opened and in tiptoed the Egg Man.

First he found the remaining chicken and put it on his head. It was his after all. Then he crept over to the grandfather clock, hoisted it onto his back and staggered outside.

By the time the
Egg Man reached
the path, sweat
was pouring
off him like
wax from
a candle.

By the time he
reached the lane
his knees
were
scraping
the ground. By the
time Nelly woke
up and howled
in fright, he was
out of his wits.

He dropped the clock. The door
fell off and out tumbled Nelly,
purple with rage and bruises.

The Egg Man ran like a hare from a hound, with his chicken flopping round his ears.

As for Nelly, she waited till Billy
was better. Then she marched him
down to the village. He had to
empty one sock to pay for the
feather hat she wanted.

He had to empty the other sock to
buy two hens, which he shooed off
into the Egg Man's field.

And his pocket bought a chicken
for tea, a bag of barley, some
onions and carrots and a handful
of freshly picked herbs.

"Friends again?" Nelly asked him.

"Friends again," said Billy.

So that night Nelly taught Billy how to cook a chicken, and while it was simmering with wonderful smells, Billy taught Nelly how to mend a grandfather clock.

Nelly put on her hat, which
made her look beautiful, and there
in the calm of the tick-tocking
evening they sat by the fire and
dined.

When the meal was over, Tricky Nelly Nickleby smiled a friendly smile at Billy the Bamboozler and said, "And what would you like, my pet, when *your* birthday comes round?"

Fun **Sprinters** for you to enjoy!

Cool as a Cucumber
Michael Morpurgo • Tor Freeman

Peter gets more than he bargained for when he starts digging the school's Jubilee vegetable garden!

No Tights for George!
June Crebbin • Tony Ross

George has to wear tights in the school play and he's in a real twist about it!

The Snow Maze
Jan Mark • Jan Ormerod

Joe discovers a secret behind the lonely gate on his way to school. But will anybody believe him?

Star Striker Titch
Martin Waddell • Russell Ayto

Little Titch wants to play a big part in the school World Cup – if only he could get on the pitch!

Tricky Nelly's Birthday Treat
Berlie Doherty • Tony Ross

It's Tricky Nelly Nickleby's birthday – and Billy the Bamboozler's got a special tricky treat in store for her!